WANTED

FEATHERS VON BEAK

For Big T and Baby R — the best partners
in crime a spaniel could wish for. — A.S

For Noah. — A.A

First published 2023 by Macmillan Children's Books
an imprint of Pan Macmillan
The Smithson, 6 Briset Street, London EC1M 5NR
EU representative: Macmillan Publishers Ireland Ltd, 1st Floor,
The Liffey Trust Centre, 117–126 Sheriff Street Upper,
Dublin 1, D01 YC43
Associated companies throughout the world.
www.panmacmillan.com

ISBN (PB): 978-1-5290-3710-4

1 3 5 7 9 8 6 4 2

A CIP catalogue record for this book is available from the British Library.

Printed in China

MIX
Paper | Supporting
responsible forestry
FSC® C116313
FSC
www.fsc.org

Andrew Sanders   Aysha Awwad

WHOSE DOG IS THIS?

BUTTONS

MACMILLAN CHILDREN'S BOOKS

Albert . . .

Yes?

. . . we do not have a dog.

I only left the room for ten minutes!
What happened?

> Well, I picked fluff out of my belly
> button for a little while . . .

Albert! *Tell me about the dog.*

> Him? He can't pick his belly button,
> Dad. He hasn't got any fingers.

Albert! Whose dog is this?

> I can't say.

Why not?

> Because he's really a
> secret agent named Jonny
> Waffles. I met him in the
> garden just now.

Albert, why would a secret agent dog be at our house?

He was trying to capture Doctor Feathers Von Beak –
a really bad goose who wants to take over the world.

A *goose?*

A *bad* goose. I just wanted to play outside, but Feathers Von Beak kept trying to get to the top-secret document in our kitchen.

Albert, we do not have a 'top-secret document' in our kitchen.

We do. It was stuck on the fridge.

You mean . . .
our shopping list?

No, Dad! It's really a secret
code! Feathers Von Beak was
after it and things really
didn't look good . . .

They didn't look good?

No. He had a super-stinky shrink ray and he tried to zap me!

A super-stinky shrink ray?

Yes, but just in time, Jonny Waffles leapt over next door's fence and knocked him flying!

Hang on – this is Buttons
from next door?
Mrs Buttercrumble's dog?

He's not really Buttons,
Dad. He's a spy.

So, the garden is a mess
because Buttons is really
a secret agent, who was
trying to stop a bad
goose from breaking into
our kitchen to steal our
shopping list, which is
really a top-secret code?

Yes.

So then, why is it such a mess . . . *in here?*

Well, Feathers Von Beak got past us and got the code!

The goose was in the house?

Yes, it was quite a struggle. We tried to
slow him down with macaroni cheese, but
he escaped back into the garden.

Wait. Are those *our* bed sheets
all over the lawn?

Well, once Feathers grabbed the code
he tried to fly off, so me and Jonny
Waffles needed a hot air balloon to
stay on his tail.

This is hard to believe, Albert.
You *flew* after him?

Yes, I don't want to worry you, but there was a bit with thunderbolts, whirlwinds and an emergency landing.

That sounds bad, Albert.

I know! And in all the confusion, Feathers Von Beak escaped in a puff of smoke!

Let me get this straight: you've kidnapped next door's dog, the bed sheets are covered in mud, the house is coated in macaroni cheese and we've only got a bag of lettuce for dinner . . .

No. We threw most of the lettuce at Feathers Von Beak, too.

. . . All because you were saving the world, *from a goose*?

Yes. But, we did it, Dad! The top-secret document is right here, safe and sound!

Albert. This is simply NOT true. Dogs are not secret agents, bed sheets cannot be used as hot air balloons and geese do not want to take over the world.

They are, they can, and they do, Dad.

Albert, if your story was true, this 'top-secret code' would be guarded like crazy.

By someone brave?

Yes.

And fearless?

Yes.

Who could keep a close eye on everything without being noticed?

Yes!

Like him!

Albert, that is enough!
We're going to take Buttons
home and then you will
help me tidy all of this
up before dinner.

Will there still be
pudding afterwards?

Albert, I love you very much.
But there is *no* chance of
pudding tonight.

We're very sorry Mrs Buttercrumble –
but here's Buttons, safe and sound.

Farewell, Jonny Waffles.

Albert!

I mean, "Bye, Buttons."

Woof.

You did well, Albert.
You did very well.